CHARLEY HARPER'S

A Partridge in a Pear Tree

An old Christmas carol which proves that it is better to give than to receive

Pomegranate

PORTLAND, OREGON

On the first day of Christmas my true love sent to me

A partridge in a pear tree

(He always gives me something unusual.)

On the second day of Christmas my true love sent to me

2 turtle doves and
A partridge in a pear tree

(The wrapping was so pretty I saved it for next Christmas.)

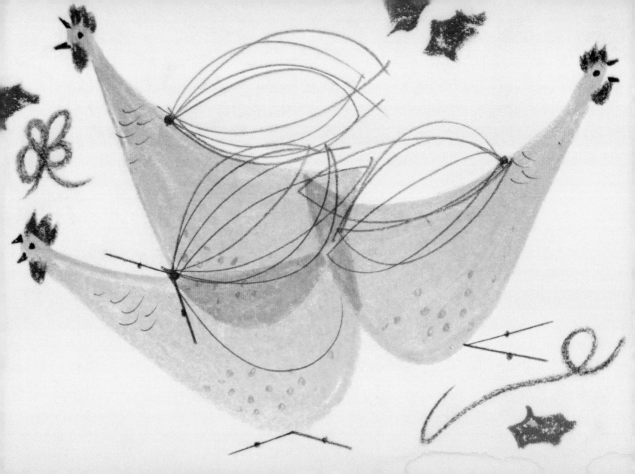

On the third day of Christmas my true love sent to me

3 French hens
2 turtle doves and
A partridge in a pear tree

(What in the world will I do with three French hens?)

On the fourth day of Christmas my true love sent to me

    4 calling birds
    3 French hens
    2 turtle doves and
    A partridge in a pear tree

(My place began to look like an aviary.)

On the fifth day of Christmas my true love sent to me

     5 golden rings
     4 calling birds
     3 French hens
     2 turtle doves and
     A partridge in a pear tree

(Seven days to go—I began to get worried.)

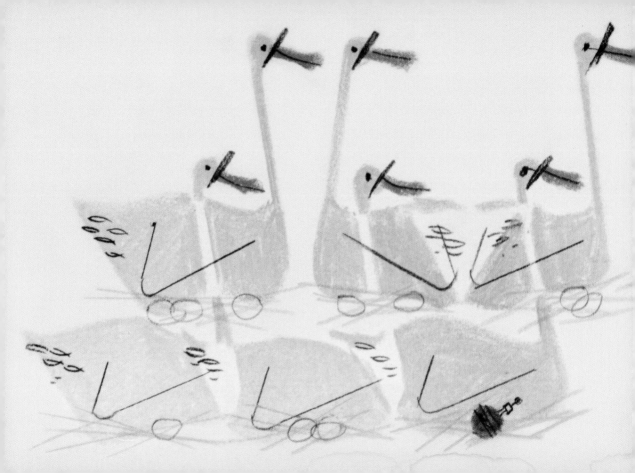

On the sixth day of Christmas my true love sent to me

6 geese a-laying
5 golden rings
4 calling birds
3 French hens
2 turtle doves and
A partridge in a pear tree

(I gave one of the French hens to my niece, Sandra.)

On the seventh day of Christmas my true love sent to me

7 swans a-swimming
6 geese a-laying
5 golden rings
4 calling birds
3 French hens
2 turtle doves and
A partridge in a pear tree

(I had to put them in the bathtub.)

On the eighth day of Christmas my true love sent to me

    8 maids a-milking
    7 swans a-swimming
    6 geese a-laying
    5 golden rings
    4 calling birds
    3 French hens
    2 turtle doves and
    A partridge in a pear tree

(I tied the cow outside.)

On the ninth day of Christmas my true love sent to me

    9 pipers piping
    8 maids a-milking
    7 swans a-swimming
    6 geese a-laying
    5 golden rings
    4 calling birds
    3 French hens
    2 turtle doves and
    A partridge in a pear tree

(I began to wish I'd never heard of Christmas.)

On the tenth day of Christmas my true love sent to me

    10 drummers drumming
    9 pipers piping
    8 maids a-milking
    7 swans a-swimming
    6 geese a-laying
    5 golden rings
    4 calling birds
    3 French hens
    2 turtle doves and
    A partridge in a pear tree

(Mrs. Jensen next door called the police.)

On the eleventh day of Christmas my true love sent to me

11 lords a-leaping
10 drummers drumming
9 pipers piping
8 maids a-milking
7 swans a-swimming
6 geese a-laying
5 golden rings
4 calling birds
3 French hens
2 turtle doves and
A partridge in a pear tree

(They knocked over the Christmas tree and frightened the cat.)

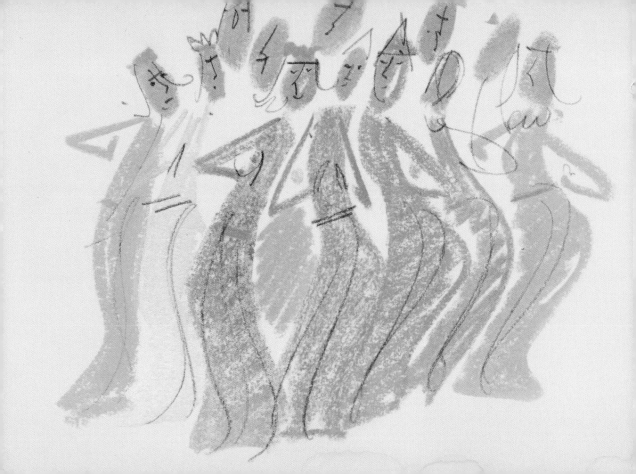

On the twelfth day of Christmas my true love sent to me

12 ladies dancing
11 lords a-leaping
10 drummers drumming
9 pipers piping
8 maids a-milking
7 swans a-swimming
6 geese a-laying
5 golden rings
4 calling birds
3 French hens
2 turtle doves and
A partridge in a pear tree

(And all I sent him was,
3 handkerchiefs
2 neckties and
A pair of socks)

On the first day after Christmas, I, carrying on though daunted,
Called the zoo, a hotel, and my love,
And said, "You dear! Just what I wanted!"

Published by Pomegranate Communications, Inc.
19018 NE Portal Way, Portland OR 97230
800 227 1428; www.pomegranate.com

Pomegranate Europe Ltd.
Unit 1, Heathcote Business Centre, Hurlbutt Road
Warwick, Warwickshire CV34 6TD, UK
[+44] 0 1926 430111
sales@pomeurope.co.uk

Library of Congress Control Number: 2014933519

To learn about new releases and special offers from Pomegranate,
please visit www.pomegranate.com and sign up for our e-mail newsletter.
For all other queries, see "Contact Us" on our home page.

Designed by Stephanie Odeh

Pomegranate Item No. A236
ISBN 978-0-7649-6851-8

Printed in China
23 22 21 20 19 18 17 16 15 14   10 9 8 7 6 5 4 3 2 1